The Green Ghost

The Green Ghost

by Marion Dane Bauer

illustrated by Peter Ferguson

A STEPPING STONE BOOK™

Random House 🏠 New York

For Bailey and Kyra—M.D.B.

Text copyright © 2008 by Marion Dane Bauer
Illustrations copyright © 2008 by Peter Ferguson

All rights reserved.
Published in the United States by Random House Children's Books, a division of Random House, Inc., New York. Originally published in hardcover in the United States by Random House Children's Books in 2008.

Random House and the colophon are registered trademarks and A Stepping Stone Book and the colophon are trademarks of Random House, Inc.

Visit us on the Web!
www.steppingstonesbooks.com
www.randomhouse.com/kids

Educators and librarians, for a variety of teaching tools, visit us at
www.randomhouse.com/teachers

The Library of Congress has cataloged the hardcover edition of this work as follows:
Bauer, Marion Dane.
The green ghost / by Marion Dane Bauer ; illustrated by Peter Ferguson.
    p. cm.
"A Stepping Stone book."
Summary: While Kaye and her parents are driving during a bad snowstorm to her grandmother's house on Christmas Eve, their car spins off the road and they take refuge in a house where Kaye meets a ghost in a green cloak.
ISBN 978-0-375-84083-8 (hardcover) — ISBN 978-0-375-94083-5 (lib. bdg.) — ISBN 978-0-375-84084-5 (pbk.)
[1. Ghosts—Fiction. 2. Christmas—Fiction. 3. Christmas trees—Fiction.]
I. Ferguson, Peter, ill. II. Title.
PZ7.B3262Gr 2008   [Fic]—dc22 2007048209

Printed in the United States of America
10 9 8 7 6 5 4 3 2 1

Contents

Chapter 1

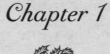

The Cloak

1938

"Papa! Look! Isn't it beautiful?" Lillian breathed the words, long and slow. In the cold air, her breath clouded the store window. She wiped it clear again with a corner of her scarf.

The cloak *was* beautiful. It was dark green wool. The hood and the cloak were lined with velvet. The velvet was a pale, silvery green.

All that green made Lillian think of a Christmas tree. Not the scraggly junipers Papa always brought home from behind the barn. It made her think of the white pine that stood at the front of the church on Christmas Eve.

Lillian's father laid his hands on her shoulders. "The cloak *is* beautiful," he agreed. "But it's hardly the thing for a girl doing farm chores."

"Oh, *Papa*!" Lillian said. But she knew he was right. The cloak hadn't been made for her . . . or for any other farmer's daughter.

"It looks so . . . warm," she said.

"Warm" wasn't exactly what she meant. But the word would have to do. "Warm" Papa could appreciate. The truth was, the cloak looked like something a lady would wear to a party. Yet it was sized for a girl. It was the perfect size for a nine-year-old girl like her.

"Yes," her father agreed gently. "It does look warm." He tugged at her scarf as he

spoke, wrapping it closer around her. He might have been reminding her of the love Mama had knit into that scarf.

Then his big hands turned her away from the store window. "We must be getting on home, Lilly," he said. "Your mama will have supper waiting. And Ben wants the barn."

Ben, their patient plow horse, stood with his head hung low. A blanket of snow covered his wide back. The snow had been falling all day. The countryside was thick with it.

Papa helped Lillian into the sleigh. He tucked a warm blanket across her lap, climbed up himself, and clucked at Ben.

Lillian looked back to check the cloak in the store window once more. Who would have thought their little general store would have anything so fine?

She tried to imagine what girl would find

it under her Christmas tree. Ruth, the minister's daughter? Maybe Clarissa, whose father owned the town bank.

Whoever it was would, no doubt, have a perfect Christmas tree, too. She would have as fine a tree as the tall white pine at church.

Lillian sighed and snuggled into her father's side.

"Are you warm, little one?" he asked.

"Warm as toast, Papa," she said.

She didn't need a green cloak. Not with Papa nearby. Still . . . she couldn't help it. She had to look back one last time. The cloak *was* beautiful! As beautiful as . . .

But the thought stuttered and stopped. Another rose inside her like a dawning sun.

So the green cloak hadn't been made for her. That didn't mean she couldn't have *anything* beautiful.

Junipers weren't the only trees on their farm. The hills that rose on every side were filled with white pines. Those trees were as beautiful as any she'd ever seen at the church. A person had only to walk a bit farther to get one.

"Papa?" she said.

"Yes, Lilly?" he replied.

"May I bring in our Christmas tree this year?"

For a long moment, her father said nothing.

Lillian held perfectly still, waiting.

Ben clop-clopped along. The harness creaked. The snow kept falling.

"Do you think you're big enough for such a task?" Papa asked at last.

"I am, Papa," she breathed. "I am!"

He nodded slowly. "All right," he said. "If it's what you want. You may bring in our tree."

Lillian clapped her mittened hands. Then she snuggled even closer to Papa.

"There's lots of juniper just behind the barn," Papa reminded her. "They're close in. And they aren't too heavy for you to carry."

"I know," Lillian told him.

But she knew something else, too. She wasn't going to settle for any ugly old juniper. She would bring home the best tree in the forest.

Wouldn't her younger brother and sister be thrilled with a tall green tree? Mama and Papa would, too. They just didn't know it yet.

Lillian looked back in the direction of the green cloak. It would never be hers. She knew that.

Still, she smiled.

Chapter 2

In the Middle
of Nowhere

The snow didn't fall. It flew. It flung itself sideways as if it never intended to land.

Kaye sat in the middle of the backseat so she could look out the windshield. All she could see, though, was the flying snow. In the headlights it became a white wall. The white wall divided at the last instant to let them through.

She checked the side windows of the car.

There she saw only darkness. She turned back to the wall of snow.

Kaye's father gripped the steering wheel hard. Next to him, her mother leaned forward. She leaned and leaned as if she could get them to Gran's faster that way.

Christmas was waiting for them at Gran's. Christmas and cookies and gifts and a ham so huge the four of them could barely make a dent in it.

A Christmas tree would be waiting, too. The tree would touch the living room ceiling, only just leaving room for the angel. It would fill one whole side of the room.

The tree would have about a thousand ornaments on it, too.

Kaye's favorite was the one shaped like a pickle. Gran always hid the glass pickle deep inside the tree for Kaye to find. When

Kaye found it, she got a special pickle gift.

At least she hoped a tree like that would be waiting.

Last year Gran had surprised everyone by saying the tree was too big, too messy, too much work. "I'm going to get one of those artificial trees next Christmas," she'd said.

All year Kaye had wondered if Gran would really do that.

It would hardly be Christmas with an artificial tree. Gran wouldn't even be able to hide a pickle ornament in one of those scrawny things.

But whether the tree was artificial or not, tomorrow was Christmas. And they still had a long way to drive. "A long, long way," Dad had barked the last time Kaye asked.

She wanted to ask again now, but she

didn't. This time Dad might say, "A long, long, *long* way."

The more the snow flew, the farther away Christmas seemed to be.

Kaye asked another question instead. "Where are we?"

But Dad didn't like that question, either. "We're in the middle of blasted nowhere," he snapped.

Mom reached back to touch Kaye's knee.

The touch was a kind of apology for Daddy's being cross. He wasn't usually cross.

"We're out in the country," Mom said. She spoke with careful cheer. Not that it helped much. Kaye could tell that her mother was working really hard to be cheerful.

Anyway, out in the country *was* the middle of nowhere. Wasn't it?

Kaye peered out the side window. There was nothing out there but darkness. Darkness and bits of flying white. There was no town. No lights. No sign that anybody else in the world was near.

They hadn't met another car for a long time. Probably everyone had gotten wherever they were going. Everyone except them.

The radio had talked all day about the big storm coming. Her dad had said they would make it to Gran's before it got too bad. But here they were.

The wind bumped against the side of the car, rocking it.

"Charles!" Mom cried in a small, breathless voice. As if Dad had made the wind. She leaned forward harder.

Kaye's father didn't answer. He just hung on to the steering wheel.

The wind bumped them again. Bump! Bump! Two sharp blows made the car shudder.

Mom didn't say anything this time. But she held on to the door.

BUMP!

The wind hit the car again. This time it slid them across the icy road. Dad turned the steering wheel. They just kept sliding.

Then there was another kind of bump.

This was the bump of the tire hitting something on the edge of the road.

And they were sliding back across the
road again. The car slid, and it turned, too . . .
like some kind of carnival ride.

It would have been fun if it hadn't been
so scary.

Mom said, "Oh!" It was just the smallest sound. She let go of the door, and her hands flew to cover her mouth. She seemed to want to stop more sounds from coming out.

Dad kept turning the wheel. And the car paid no attention at all.

They slid and spun. First they spun until

they were facing backward. Then they spun until they faced front again. Front didn't look much different from back.

In the headlights the snow kept coming at them. It sped toward them like millions of white bullets.

The car made another turn, but partway through it went bump again. And bump! And BUMP!

Now the car was sliding down a small, steep hill. And suddenly everything stopped.

Everything except the snow. It kept flying. And the wind kept moaning.

All else was silent.

For a moment, they sat perfectly still. There was nothing to see except flying snow.

Then Kaye's parents turned to look at

her. They turned at the same time. Their heads could have been pulled by the same string.

"Are you all right?" they asked in one voice.

When Kaye opened her mouth to answer, no sound came out. She nodded instead.

Mom looked at Dad. "Where are we?" she asked.

"Out in the country," he answered. "In the middle of blasted nowhere."

And then, strange as it might seem, they both laughed.

Chapter 3

The Light

"It's not so bad," Dad said. "We'll get out of here. Just hold tight." He put the car in reverse and pressed the gas pedal.

The wheels spun. The car settled more deeply into the ditch.

He tried again, more gently this time. The car didn't move.

He tried rocking, forward, back, forward, back. Nothing. They weren't going anywhere.

Mom was quiet. But her hands were clenched into fists.

Kaye looked down. Her hands were fists, too.

"Well," Dad said at last. "I'd better get out and have a look."

When he opened his door, the wind roared more loudly. When he stepped out, the storm swallowed him.

Kaye's teeth began to chatter. She wasn't cold exactly. At least she didn't think she was. She was just—

Dad jerked the door open and tumbled back in. He had snow everywhere. He even had snow in his eyebrows!

"We're well and truly stuck," he said. "We won't get out of here without a tow."

"What will we do?" Mom asked.

Kaye waited. What *would* they do?

Mom was waiting, too.

Dad didn't answer.

And that was when Kaye saw it. A small, pale face appeared at her window. No . . . it wasn't a face. It was just a light. A lighted face?

That didn't make sense.

But there it was again. A pale face floated outside her window.

"Look!" Kaye said.

Her parents both turned to look.

"What?" Dad asked.

"Can't you see?" Kaye asked. "It's a . . ." At the last instant she decided not to say "face." What face would be out here in the storm? "It's a light," she said instead.

"I can't see any light," her dad said.

"I can't, either," her mom said.

The light bobbed outside her window

again. It seemed to be calling to her.

"There!" Kaye put her hand against the window. If the glass hadn't been in the way, she could have touched it. "It's right there!"

And before her parents could say again that there was no light, she pushed the door open. When she had it open just a bit, the wind yanked it wide. She tumbled out. For an instant, the driving snow blinded her.

When she could make out the light again, it was farther away.

It might have been the moon, except it was much too close for the moon.

It might have been a face, except it was too bright for any face.

Kaye moved toward it.

"Kaye!" her mother cried. "Get back in the car!"

"Now!" her father ordered.

The light—or the face, whatever it was—
called to her. Not with a voice. The only
"voice" she could hear was the wind's. Still,
the light called as clearly as if it had said,
"Come!"

"But I see a light!" Kaye tossed the
words back over her shoulder.

"What light?" her father demanded. He was out of the car now.

"It's there," she said. "Right over there." And she started toward it again.

She felt her father grab at her jacket, but she pulled away.

"Kaye!" her mother called.

Kaye watched the light. She could almost touch it. And then she couldn't.

It must not have been as close as it seemed. It couldn't be far, though.

She began to run.

She heard her parents stumbling after her. The snow was deep. The wind howled. The wind unwound the scarf from her neck and flung it away.

Kaye paid no attention. She just kept going.

Someone was calling her.

Chapter 4

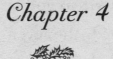

Don't Go Far

1938

"I wanna go, Lillian." Elsa jumped up and down. Her dark curls bobbed with each jump. "I wanna go! Pretty please?"

Lillian shook her head at her three-year-old sister. She *always* wanted to go where Lillian went.

"You can't, Elsa," she said. "I'm going to get our Christmas tree. And I have to go a long, long way . . . deep into the woods."

"You don't need to go far, Lillian," Mama said. She opened the oven door, and the kitchen filled with the warm smell of bread. "You know Papa always gets our trees from behind the barn."

Lillian sighed. "I know, Mama. But I want—"

"See, Lilly. See!" Elsa interrupted. "We don't need to go far!" She was jumping again.

Lillian spoke over Elsa's bouncing head. "Those old junipers don't even smell good," she said. "And they're prickly. Last year, by the time we had it decorated, my arms were all in a rash."

Lillian's mother tipped a crusty loaf out of its pan. Her cheeks were flushed from the heat of the oven. "I don't know why you insist on going, anyway, Lilly. Your papa always gets a tree for us. You know he does."

"But I want a *pretty* tree," Lillian cried. She loved her papa, of course. He was the best papa in the world. But he didn't seem to care about pretty . . . except when he'd picked Mama, of course.

Her mother sighed. "If you must go, then take Elsa with you. She needs some fresh air. She hasn't been outside the house this live-long day."

Lillian opened her mouth to object, but stopped herself. Mama looked tired.

"All right," she said. If she had to take someone, she would rather have taken her little brother. Isaac was six, not such a baby. But he was out in the barn, helping Papa with chores. And Elsa was the one Mama needed rest from.

"Come on, Elsa," Lillian said. She put on a cheerful voice. "Get your coat."

Elsa dashed to get it down from its peg.

"Now don't go far," Mama warned. "It's cold out there and getting colder. And it will be dark soon."

"We won't," Lillian promised. *Just far enough*, she said to herself. But she wrapped Elsa's scarf extra tight.

Elsa sprang out the door and ran ahead of Lillian. She stopped when they reached the unappealing gray junipers.

"Not these," Lillian told her. "Don't you want a *pretty* tree?"

Elsa nodded. Lillian took her sister's hand as they started up the hill.

Mama was right. The day *had* turned cold. The sky had cleared and the woods lay in snowy silence. The snow squeaked beneath their boots.

Elsa broke away and ran up to a young

tree. It wasn't a white pine, though. "Here's one!" she cried. "Here's our Christmas tree!"

Lillian shook her head. "The needles are too short," she said.

Soon Elsa pointed to a long-needled one. But it had grown up close to another tree. One side was completely flat.

"No," Lillian said. "Not that one."

Next Elsa found one with a crooked trunk.

Lillian smiled. Her little sister seemed to have their father's eye for beauty. Or perhaps she just felt sorry for the ugly ones.

"No," Lillian said. "We're looking for the most spectacular tree in the forest."

Elsa stopped walking. "I didn't know trees wore spectacles," she said.

Lillian laughed. She shifted the small saw she carried and reached for her sister's hand.

She could feel Elsa's delicate bones through the mittens their mother had knit.

"Let's go just a little bit farther," Lillian said.

"Just a little bit farther," Elsa agreed.

They trudged on.

Chapter 5

The Ugliest Tree

Kaye bumped into the porch steps before she saw the house. There was her light! It poured through a window onto the porch. The wind and the snow had just been playing tricks to make it seem closer.

"Here!" she called to her parents. "We're here!" She stumbled up the steps.

Her parents caught up with her on the

porch. "It's a house!" her father cried. "How did you see it?"

"I saw the light," she said. "I told you."

They found the door together.

Dad knocked. They waited. He knocked again.

Wasn't anyone home?

Kaye shivered. The wind seemed to blow right through her. There must be icicles hanging from her bones.

Dad took off his glove and knocked again with his bare knuckles.

A hand pulled back a curtain in the door's window. A face appeared on the other side.

It wasn't a lighted face, though. Just a face.

At last the door cracked open. A grandmotherly woman appeared in the crack.

Her hair stood in white corkscrews all over her head.

"My goodness!" she exclaimed. "Where did you folks come from?" She opened the door wider. "Come in! Come in! You must be frozen stiff!"

They all clumped in and stopped just inside the door. Kaye looked at her parents. They looked like snow people. She looked down at herself. She was a snow person, too.

Snow clung to her coat. It had burrowed inside her collar. It had sifted down inside her boots.

Her nose was numb. Her fingers and toes were, too. The warm kitchen air stung her cheeks.

Weren't they lucky, though, that she had seen the light?

Kaye's father told the woman about their car being in the ditch. He told her about the way the wind had bumped them off the road. "We're going to need a tow," he said.

"What a thing!" she cried. "And on such a night! Now, you folks just take off your coats. We'll get you warm. Then we'll see what we can do."

She bustled around, taking their coats. "I'm Elsa," she told them. She hung the coats on wooden pegs by the door. "That's what everybody around here calls me—just Elsa."

She was short and round. Kaye's own grandma was tall and skinny. But Elsa reminded Kaye of her grandma, anyway. Gran was cheerful in the same bustling way.

When Elsa smiled, her face bloomed into friendly wrinkles. She was clearly happy to have a strange family in her kitchen.

And they were certainly happy to be inside a warm house.

They were happy for the wild-rice-and-chicken soup Elsa warmed for them, too. And for the buttered toast she made to go with the soup. The toast filled the kitchen with a rich, nutty smell.

While they ate, Elsa talked. She told them about the farm. It had been in her family for generations, she said. She told them how she and her brother, Isaac, had farmed it together. But Isaac had died, she said, and now the land was rented out.

She didn't say she was lonely, but Kaye could tell she was.

She did say that it was surely an angel who had brought them to her on this stormy night.

When she said that, about the angel, Kaye thought about the face outside her car window. But no, that hadn't been a face. It was just the light shining from the house. That had to be what it was.

When Elsa finally paused for breath, Dad mentioned their stuck car again.

Elsa nodded. "I can get one of my neighbors to bring a tractor and pull you out. That's no trouble," she said. "But I don't think it's a good idea."

Dad's eyebrows went up.

"This storm is a bad one," she explained. "And until it blows itself out, they won't plow the roads. So even if somebody got you out, you'd be right back in the ditch again. Or worse."

When she said "Or worse," Mom and Dad looked at one another across the table. Kaye could tell they were thinking about what the "worse" might be.

"Now, I think you should call your family," Elsa said. "Let them know you're safe. Tell them you'll be here with me until you can travel again. That's going to take a bit of time. So tomorrow we'll all have Christmas right here."

Christmas! Kaye hadn't thought about Christmas once since the car had started spinning.

Christmas! They were going to spend Christmas *here*?

For the first time, she looked around. Really looked. The kitchen was plain and neat and bright.

A teakettle hummed softly on the stove. A red-and-white-checked cloth covered the table. The good smell of toast still hung in the air. Everything was friendly the way Elsa was friendly.

But still, they couldn't have Christmas here!

It wasn't just that Elsa wasn't Kaye's grandma. What about the gifts Gran bought all year long and stashed away in a closet waiting for Christmas? What about the ham? What about the pickle ornament?

What about the tree?

Kaye leapt from the table and moved

to look through the living room doorway.

She had been afraid Elsa wouldn't have a tree at all. But there it stood in the corner of the living room. A Christmas tree. If it could be called a Christmas tree.

It was small and scraggly. It was more gray than green. And Kaye could tell, even from the doorway, that it didn't have that good evergreen smell.

The next words popped out before she even knew she was going to say them.

"What an ugly tree!" she said.

"Kaye!" her mother cried. "That's—"

But before Mom could say "rude," Elsa interrupted. She laughed. She just tipped her head back and laughed and laughed.

"Never mind," she said. "Kaye's right! It's a family tradition . . . an ugly tree for Christmas. They're junipers. They grow out behind the barn."

"I'm sorry," Kaye said. "I didn't mean—"

Though, of course, she *had* meant it. Even with the lights and the glass balls, it was just about the ugliest tree she had ever seen. And what kind of a family tradition was that, anyway . . . to have an ugly tree for Christmas?

Elsa waved her apology away. Still, Kaye was sorry she'd said it. She was especially sorry because Elsa didn't fool her. Beneath the laughter, Kaye could see sadness in the old woman's eyes.

But that was nothing compared to the sadness Kaye felt. She'd worried all year about what kind of tree Gran was going to have. Would she really have an artificial one? It would spoil Christmas if she did.

But nothing could spoil Christmas more than being stuck here with no gifts and no Gran and this dumb old juniper from behind the barn.

Nothing!

Chapter 6

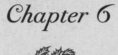

The Perfect Tree

1938

They walked and walked. Lillian knew she should turn around, but she didn't. As soon as she found the right tree, they would go back.

Elsa's feet dragged. Lillian was getting tired, too. But her sister didn't complain, so she kept going.

"We'll find it very soon," she promised.

"Soon," Elsa agreed. But she sighed. She

lifted her tiny shoulders almost to her ears and let them fall again.

At last they broke out of a dense stand of trees into a clearing. And there it was—exactly what Lillian had been looking for.

It was the most beautiful tree she had ever seen! Even nicer than the one at church.

It was a white pine. The needles were long. Lillian could tell they were soft before she even touched them. The whole tree was a rich, deep green that shaded into silver. It was full and beautifully shaped, too. No other tree had crowded close or risen higher to cut off the sun.

"This is the one." Lillian dropped Elsa's hand. "This is the very one!"

Elsa tipped her head back and gazed up and up at the tree. "It's so tall," she said.

"I know," Lillian said. "That's what makes it so wonderful!"

Elsa said nothing more. She just plopped down in the snow to wait. And Lillian set to work. She had to take off a few of the lower limbs first. Once she could reach in easily, she began sawing at the trunk.

At first the saw kept slipping. It wouldn't bite through the bark. But Lillian didn't stop trying until it took hold.

"You're coming home with us," she told the tree. "Our family's going to have the most beautiful Christmas tree in the whole valley." And she set to pulling and pushing at the saw.

Lillian worked for a while. Then she stopped to catch her breath. She stepped back to gaze up at the tree again. It *was* tall. It must be twice as tall as Papa. Maybe more.

Was that too tall? Would it be too heavy to bring home? Would it even fit in their farm-house?

Lillian checked Elsa. She sat in the snow, her arms wrapped around her knees.

"Are you all right?" Lillian asked.

"C–c-cold," Elsa said.

"Oh, Elsa, I'm sorry." Lillian dropped the saw and went to her little sister. Lillian gathered Elsa into her arms. She tipped Elsa's chin up so she could see her face.

Elsa's cheeks and nose had been cheerfully red a few minutes ago. Now they were white.

"I shouldn't have brought you so far," Lillian said.

Elsa snuggled into her arms. "It's a b–b-beautiful tree," she whispered.

"Yes, it is." Lillian looked up to the very top. The sky beyond was no longer a bright blue. The color seemed to have drained from it the way it had from Elsa's face.

But still . . . the tree *was* perfect. Even Papa

would love it! "Do you think you could wait a little longer?" she asked Elsa. "Just until I can get it cut?"

Elsa nodded.

"Here," Lillian said. "I'll keep myself warm with sawing." She took off her coat and wrapped it around her sister. If only she had that green cloak. That would have kept Elsa warmer still.

Elsa snuggled into the extra coat. Lillian leapt up and went back to her work. She sawed and sawed. The blade bit deeper. But when she stood and pushed on the trunk, the tree didn't even sway.

Lillian pulled harder on the saw. She pushed back hard, too. On the next pull, the saw caught. She tugged, but she couldn't budge it.

She tried to pull it out so she could start

again on the other side. But that didn't work, either. The blade was firmly stuck in the trunk.

Lillian shivered. She was cold now, too. She should stop and take Elsa home. She could bring Papa back tomorrow to get the tree.

If she could find it again tomorrow.

That was the problem. She could find her way home easily enough. The wooded hills sloped down to the river and to their farm. So she had only to go down. But coming back to find one tree in the deep woods would be much harder.

No. If she was going to get this tree, it had to be now.

Lillian bent again to the saw.

Chapter 7

Into the Woods

When Kaye opened her eyes, a girl was sitting next to her on the bed.

"Oh!" Kaye said. She sat up.

At first she thought, *I've seen this girl before.* Then she knew she couldn't have.

The girl smiled at her.

"Where did you—?" Kaye started to say.

But the girl interrupted her. "Are you ready?" she asked. Her pale face glowed softly from under the hood of a dark cloak.

It occurred to Kaye later that she should have been frightened. It was certainly odd to wake up in the middle of the night to find a strange girl sitting on her bed.

Kaye wasn't scared, though. Maybe because the glowing face looked so friendly.

"Are you ready?" the girl asked again.

"Ready for what?" Kaye asked.

"To get a Christmas tree," the girl said.

"A big one?" Kaye said.

"Of course," the girl answered. "Big, and beautiful, too."

Kaye's feet were on the floor instantly.

But even as she stood, second thoughts flooded in. "Now?" she asked. "It's the middle of the night!"

"The middle of Christmas Eve night," the girl pointed out.

Kaye understood. What was the point of a tree if it wasn't there on Christmas morning? "Okay," she said. "Where are we going?"

This time the girl didn't answer. She just

floated out of the room. Well, no. She didn't float. Not really. She must have walked. But she walked so smoothly, so silently, it seemed like floating.

Kaye pulled on her jeans and sweatshirt. Then she followed the girl. Kaye found her waiting downstairs in the kitchen.

"Get your coat," the girl said. "You breathing folks get cold, don't you?"

You breathing folks! What other kind of folks were there?

Still, Kaye pulled her jacket down from the peg where Elsa had hung it. She put on her hat and boots, too. Her boots were fleece-lined, so it didn't matter that her feet were bare.

She looked for her scarf and then remembered. The wind had stolen it on the way to Elsa's house.

And that made her think of the storm. Was it still raging out there? Did she want to go outside?

But the girl waited beside the door, so Kaye opened it. The girl moved out ahead and Kaye followed.

She stopped on the edge of the porch, amazed. The storm had blown itself out. The night was as still now as it had been blustery before. A round, creamy moon rode high in the sky. The world was sketched in shades of black and white.

Even the old barn across the way looked beautiful under its sparkling blanket of snow.

Kaye stepped down from the porch. The snow lay everywhere, deep and untouched.

"Where are we going?" she called to the girl, who had gone ahead.

"Not far," the girl called back.

For the first time, Kaye hesitated. Should she go off with this strange girl? What if her parents woke and found her gone?

But she couldn't let the girl get away.

Besides, they wouldn't be at Elsa's much longer. The storm had stopped. The plows would come through. A farmer would pull their car out. She and her parents could have Christmas breakfast with Elsa. And maybe the girl would be there, too? Then they could go on to Gran's.

Wouldn't it be nice, though, to leave Elsa with a beautiful tree? Family tradition or not, nobody needed a scraggly old juniper for Christmas.

Kaye hurried to catch up.

"What's your name?" Kaye called after the girl. If she was going to follow this stranger, she should at least know her name.

"Lillian," the girl called back.

Lillian, Kaye thought. *I like that!*

And lifting her feet high to make her way through the deep snow, she followed Lillian into the woods.

Chapter 8

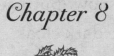

The Tree

Lillian led the way. No matter how fast Kaye walked, the girl always stayed a short distance ahead.

Kaye followed her through the scrubby trees behind the barn. She followed her into the moon-shadowed forest.

Here the land sloped up sharply. Lillian didn't slow her pace.

Kaye's legs began to ache from walking

in such deep snow. But she kept her eyes fastened on the dark cloak.

"Do you have a saw or ax?" she called to Lillian. "To cut the tree?"

"We don't need one," Lillian answered.

A shiver ran through Kaye. Not from the cold, exactly, just from . . . She wasn't sure what it was from.

What did Lillian plan to do, pull a tree out by its roots?

Again Kaye quickened her pace, trying to catch up. Again the distance between her and the strange girl never seemed to shorten.

If the moon hadn't been so bright, Kaye wouldn't have been able to follow at all. With her back turned, Lillian's glowing face was hidden. She became little more than a moving shadow.

"Could you slow down, please?" Kaye called. Her heart was beginning to pound. Her breath stuttered.

"Sure," Lillian said.

But if she actually slowed, Kaye couldn't tell.

What if this girl was playing a trick on her? What if she was trying to get Kaye lost in the woods? Could she find her way back to Elsa's alone if she had to?

Just when Kaye was beginning to think the worst, Lillian called cheerfully, "We're here!" And she stopped walking.

Huffing, Kaye caught up. She stopped beside Lillian and looked around to see where "here" might be.

They had stepped through a thick line of trees and now stood in a clearing. At the center of the clearing rose a magnificent pine. It was, in fact, one of the most beautiful trees Kaye had ever seen. It had long, soft-looking needles. It had enormous pinecones decorated with snow. It was perfectly shaped, too. No other tree had grown close to spoil its shape.

The pine rose and rose and rose, perhaps a hundred feet into the air. Kaye had to tip her head back to see the top. The round moon seemed to have come to rest there.

"It's . . . it's beautiful," she said.

"Yes," Lillian said. "It's always been beautiful." And she touched the tip of a branch.

Kaye stared, first at Lillian's glowing face, then at the tree. Then she looked back at Lillian again. Surely she didn't think they could take a tree like this back to the house! If Gran's trees had always been big, this one was humongous.

It was much too tall to fit inside any house. And it would be too heavy to carry, too.

Besides, as she had already pointed out, they didn't have a saw or an ax. Lillian had said they didn't need one.

But that was when Kaye noticed it for the first time. A rusty saw poked out from the tree's trunk. Clearly, many years before, someone had tried to cut this tree. And clearly, too, the tree had won. It had simply grown around the tool.

Kaye knelt and touched the saw. She tugged on it once. It didn't budge. She looked back into Lillian's glowing face.

"It's stuck," Kaye said. "And anyway, the tree's too big. Don't you think it's too big?" She spoke gently as though to someone much younger than she was, someone who might not understand.

"No," Lillian said. "It's just right. Elsa will love it."

Kaye said it again: "But this tree's too big. And the saw is stuck. See?" She tugged on it again to show Lillian just how stuck it was.

"It doesn't matter," Lillian said. "Just tell her. Bring her here and tell her."

Kaye stood up. "Tell her what?" she asked.

"Tell her I'm here," Lillian said.

And even as she spoke, Lillian stepped back toward the line of trees and disappeared. She simply vanished.

Kaye gasped. For a few heartbeats, she stood in the silence of the snow-filled woods. Alone. She didn't know when she had ever been so alone.

"Lillian," she called. "Lillian!" But she knew. There was no point in calling. There was no point in running after her, either. Lillian was gone.

Kaye trembled. She shook from head to foot. Even her teeth clacked together.

A sound came from her throat, but she wasn't crying. She certainly didn't mean to be crying.

How could this girl have called her from her bed and then left her here . . . in the night . . . in the woods?

Kaye tried to calm herself so she could think. Lillian expected her to go back. Lillian wanted her to take a message to Elsa, so she clearly thought Kaye would know how to find the house.

The sound from her throat kept growing louder. Kaye covered her mouth to make it stop.

And then she spotted the footprints. The full moon rode high in the sky. She could see footprints clearly in the snow.

The snow was new. All Kaye had to do was follow the footprints back to Elsa's house.

She took a deep breath and swallowed her tears. Then she turned and set her foot in the first print. She trudged forward through the fresh, deep snow.

It was only when she was halfway back to the house that she realized . . .

The footprints she followed . . . there was only one set. Only her own footprints showed!

That meant Lillian had to be a . . .

Kaye couldn't say the word. Not even in her mind. But it rang through her as if she were a bell.

And the next thing she knew, she was running . . . fast. She was running and stumbling through the trees and down the hill toward Elsa's house.

Chapter 9

The Cloak

1938

Lillian stopped sawing to look over at her sister.

Elsa had tipped over onto her side. She lay curled in the snow like a kitten. But she didn't have a kitten's warm fur. Even with two coats, she was shivering so hard that her teeth chattered.

Lillian rushed to her sister's side again. "Oh, Elsa, I'm sorry," she cried. "We'll go back. We'll go back home right now."

But Elsa didn't answer. She didn't move, either. Lillian lifted her, but she couldn't get Elsa to stand. Her legs were rubbery.

If Papa had been here, he could have carried Elsa back easily. Even Mama could carry her. Elsa was short for her age, but she was a chubby little girl. Lillian could lift her, but she couldn't get far with such a load.

Lillian considered leaving her and running back home for help. But Elsa looked so tiny lying there. So tiny and so cold. How could she leave her? And what if she couldn't find her way back to this spot quickly enough?

So Lillian did the only thing she could think of. She gathered Elsa into her arms. Then she carried her into the shelter of the tree she had been trying to cut. The limbs were thick, so there was little snow near the trunk. Lillian laid Elsa on the bed of soft pine needles.

Lillian tucked both coats more closely around her. Then she lay down behind Elsa and pulled her close. She wrapped her own body around Elsa as tightly as she could.

"It's all right," Lillian whispered. "It's all right. Papa will come." And she breathed her warm breath into her sister's neck.

Elsa cuddled in closer.

Lillian lay perfectly still, holding her little sister.

After a time, Elsa quit shivering. Lillian was glad of that. She was so glad she hardly noticed that she was the one shivering now. Later, though, she did notice when her own shivering stopped.

She must be getting warmer. She *was* getting warmer. She was certain of that. And in

that gathering warmth, Lillian slipped into sleep.

She dreamed that Papa was coming. She had always known he would come!

Papa *was* coming. In his arms he carried a woolen cloak as richly green as any pine tree.

Chapter 10

Lots of Room

"Ghost!" Kaye cried.

She banged through the door into the kitchen. Without shedding her coat or boots, she clattered up the stairs. She burst into the bedroom where her parents were sleeping.

"Ghost!" she cried again. "She's a ghost! I know it!"

Her father sat up. His hair poked out in every direction, the way it always did when he slept. "What?" he cried. His arm reached to pull her into a tight hug. "Kaye, what's wrong?"

"What is it, sweetheart?" Her mother sat up, too, and laid a hand on Kaye's back. "Did you have a bad dream?"

"It wasn't a dream," Kaye cried. She shook herself free of her parents. "She was real. She was a ghost, and she was real!"

But her mother wasn't interested in the ghost. She touched Kaye's jacket, her cheeks. "Kaye!" she cried. "You're cold. You've been outside!"

"Is something wrong?" It was Elsa, standing in the doorway to the bedroom. "Is she all right?"

And so Kaye explained about waking to find the girl sitting on her bed, about following her into the woods, about the enormous tree.

"She wants you to see it," she said to Elsa. "That's why she came to me. So I could take you to see the tree."

Elsa stood very still, saying nothing.

"It's a special tree," Kaye explained. "It's

a Christmas tree . . . for you. A really beautiful one." Kaye didn't know when she had begun crying again. She swiped at the tears running down her cheeks. Elsa had to believe her. She just had to!

Kaye could see the adults exchanging looks over her head. *We know this is nonsense,* the looks said. *But she's upset. Maybe she'll calm down if we do this thing she wants.*

"Okay," her father said very slowly. "Why don't you show us?"

Kaye wiped away her tears.

Before they left, Elsa made hot chocolate for everyone. "To warm your bones," she said. While they drank it, she whipped up a coffee cake and put it into the oven.

Then they put on their coats. When they stepped out onto the porch, the sun was just rising behind the trees on the hill. The slanting rays gave the fresh snow a rosy glow.

"That way." Kaye pointed to her footprints, the ones going and the ones coming back. There were still no other prints beside them.

She set out, and the adults followed close behind.

When Kaye reached the line of trees at the edge of the clearing, she stopped and took Elsa's hand.

"It's right up here," she said.

Elsa nodded.

And so they stepped together into the clearing.

Before them in the sweet morning light, the tree rose . . . and rose . . . and rose. Its limbs stretched out on every side. Snow lay on the branches.

"It's for you," Kaye told her.

Elsa gripped Kaye's hand tightly. "How did you know?" she asked. "This tree . . . this . . ." But she said no more.

"I told you," Kaye said. "Lillian brought me here last night. She wanted—"

Elsa released her hand. She stepped away. "Lillian?" she whispered. "You saw Lillian?"

Kaye nodded. Hadn't she said the girl's name before? Maybe she hadn't.

"What was she wearing?" Elsa cried. "If you saw Lillian, tell me what she had on."

"A cloak," Kaye answered. "She was wearing a long cloak . . . with . . . with a hood."

Elsa gasped, but the question hadn't gone out of her eyes. "What color?" she demanded. "What color was it?"

Kaye tried hard to think. In the moon-
light, nothing had any color. Everything
was shades of black and white.

But then she remembered that first
moment. She remembered opening her eyes

to find a girl sitting beside her on the bed. A
light had shone from the hall, and she'd
been able to see color.

"The cloak was green," she said. "It was
a rich, beautiful green . . . just like this tree."

Elsa burst into tears.

Kaye stood before her, silent and amazed. Had she done something wrong?

Finally Elsa explained. She told how her sister, Lillian, had taken her that long-ago winter afternoon to cut a special tree. "A spectacular one," she said. How Lillian had put her own coat on Elsa to keep her warm. How she'd finally given up and cuddled Elsa to warm her.

Elsa could remember going to sleep in her sister's arms, though she didn't know until their father came that Lillian wouldn't wake again.

Papa, Elsa said, had gone into town and bought the green cloak Lillian had wanted so much. They buried her in it.

"When I was a girl," she said, "Lillian visited me every year, right around Christmas. She'd make a joke about the ugly juniper Papa always cut for the house. And then she and I would walk out together to see this tree."

She tipped her head back to see the tree's tip. "We'd bring strings of cranberries and popcorn to decorate it. We'd put suet and peanut butter on it for the birds. Every year she came . . . until I was about thirteen. I suppose I thought myself quite grown up that year. Too old to believe in . . ."

She shook her head. "She never came again," she said. "I quit visiting the tree. I thought she was the one who'd left me."

"No," Kaye said softly. "She said to tell you she's here."

Elsa cried again. Only this time she was laughing, too.

"Oh my," she said at last. "I think it's

time for breakfast. My coffee cake must be ready to come out of the oven."

And they all started back down the hill, following the footprints once more. There were multiple prints now, jumbled and crisscrossed.

The group walked in a peaceful silence. Kaye knew her parents would have questions later. That was all right. She would answer them as best she could.

But as they stepped out of the trees into the bright sunshine, she had an idea. It was a perfectly wonderful idea.

"Elsa," she said, "will you come with us to my gran's?" Then she added, before Elsa had a chance to answer, "She'll have a huge . . ." Before she could say "tree," she stopped herself. She didn't know what kind of tree Gran would have this year. Maybe it would be tiny. Maybe it would even be one of those artificial ones.

But what did it matter?

She started again. "You'd like my gran," she said. "I know you would. And her Christmas is always huge. There'd be plenty of room for all of us."

Kaye glanced at her parents as she spoke. *Was it all right?* She knew she should have asked them first.

To her relief, they were both nodding. "That's a wonderful idea!" her mother said. "You must come!"

"Yes," agreed Kaye's father.

"I'd love to," Elsa said, still crying, still smiling. "Yes, I'd love to."

And Kaye twirled, clapping her hands.

When she had to stop for breath, she looked back toward the woods.

There, at the edge of the trees, stood a girl. She wore a green cape, as green as a pine tree, with a silvery green velvet lining.

She waved to Kaye.

And though she was too far away to see for sure, Kaye could have sworn that Lillian was crying and smiling, too.

About the Author

Marion Dane Bauer is the author of more than sixty books for children, including the Newbery Honor–winning *On My Honor*. She has also won the Kerlan Award for her collected work. Marion's first Stepping Stone book, *The Blue Ghost*, was named to the Texas Bluebonnet Award 2007–2008 Master List. Marion teaches writing and is on the faculty of the Vermont College Master of Fine Arts in Writing for Children and Young Adults program.

Marion has nine grandchildren and lives in Eden Prairie, Minnesota.

If you liked
The Green Ghost
you won't want to miss these stories!

The Blue Ghost

The light moved closer. It grew larger as it approached.

It had a shape now . . . or almost a shape. It seemed to form a person, a woman. One second Liz could see her clearly. She could make out the long, old-fashioned dress. She could see the woman's hair was pulled back in a bun. Then the figure wavered like smoke in a puff of wind.

The Red Ghost

Jenna pushed the blanket back again. She swung her feet out of the bed. But she stopped before she stood up. She just stopped and sat there, thinking.

The doll was in her closet, too. Miss Tate's doll. The one she was going to give to Quinn. It was all wrapped up, taped up, even decorated with a red bow. But it was in there.

And suddenly Jenna didn't want to open the closet door.

The Secret of the Painted House

Emily was about to turn back when she glimpsed something white. What was it? Even staring hard, she couldn't tell. White seemed an unlikely color to be part of a tree or bush. She made her way toward it.

She didn't know what to expect. Certainly not what she found.

A house stood in a small clearing. It was a real house, but small. Maybe it was a child's playhouse. A girl her size could walk right into it. A grown-up would have to duck to get in through the door. The walls were painted white. The roof, the door, and the shutters at the windows were a rich royal blue.